This edition published by Parragon in 2012
Parragon
Queen Street House
4 Queen Street
Bath BA1 1HE, UK
www.parragon.com

Copyright © Parragon Books Ltd 2011

ISBN 978-1-4454-7795-4

Printed in China

Little Red Riding Hood

Retold by Gaby Goldsack

Illustrated by Dubravka Kolanovic

PaRragon

Bath • New York • Singapore • Hong Kong • Cologne • Delhi
Melbourne • Amsterdam • Johannesburg • Auckland • Shenzhen

Once upon a time, there was a little girl who lived with her mommy in a cottage on the edge of a big forest.

Whenever the little girl went outside to play, she wore a beautiful red cloak that her grandma had made for her. It had a big red hood, so everyone called the little girl ...

Little Red Riding Hood.

One day, Little Red Riding Hood's mommy asked her to take a basket of food to Grandma.

"Grandma isn't feeling well," Mommy explained, "and I'm sure she'd love to see you."

Grandma lived on the other side of the forest, so Mommy drew a map on a piece of paper so that Little Red Riding Hood wouldn't get lost.

"And remember, don't talk to any strangers along the way," said Mommy, helping Little Red Riding Hood into her cloak.

Little Red Riding Hood took the basket of food and skipped into the forest.

On the way, Little Red Riding Hood saw some beautiful blue flowers.

"Grandma might like these," she thought. As she bent down to pick a handful of the flowers, she didn't realize someone else was in the forest ...

"Hello, little girl,"

said a deep, growly voice.

Little Red Riding Hood jumped
with fright.

A big wolf peered out from behind one of the trees.

"Oh, hello," replied Little Red Riding Hood, smiling back at the wolf. She had already forgotten her mommy's warning.

"Where are you going?" growled the wolf.

"I'm visiting my sick grandma who lives on the other side of the forest," Little Red Riding Hood explained.

"Ah, what a kind girl you are," smiled the wolf, showing off his razor-sharp teeth.

Just then the wolf's tummy gave a LOUD, rumbly grumble.

"What was that?" asked Little Red Riding Hood.

"Just some thunder over the hills," said the sneaky, hungry wolf, as he ran away as fast as he could to Grandma's cottage.

The hungry wolf peered through Grandma's window and saw the old lady in bed.

With a loud howl, the wolf dashed into the cottage and gobbled up Grandma in one large gulp!

Then the wolf put on Grandma's spare nightcap and glasses, clambered into her bed, and pulled the quilt up to his chin.

Now all he had to do was wait for Little Red Riding Hood to arrive.

When Little Red Riding Hood reached the cottage, she was surprised to find the front door wide open.

"Grandma!" she called. "Are you there?"

"I'm in the bedroom," replied the wolf in a strange, wobbly voice.

Little Red Riding Hood went into the bedroom and gasped in surprise when she saw her grandma. She looked sort of ... different.

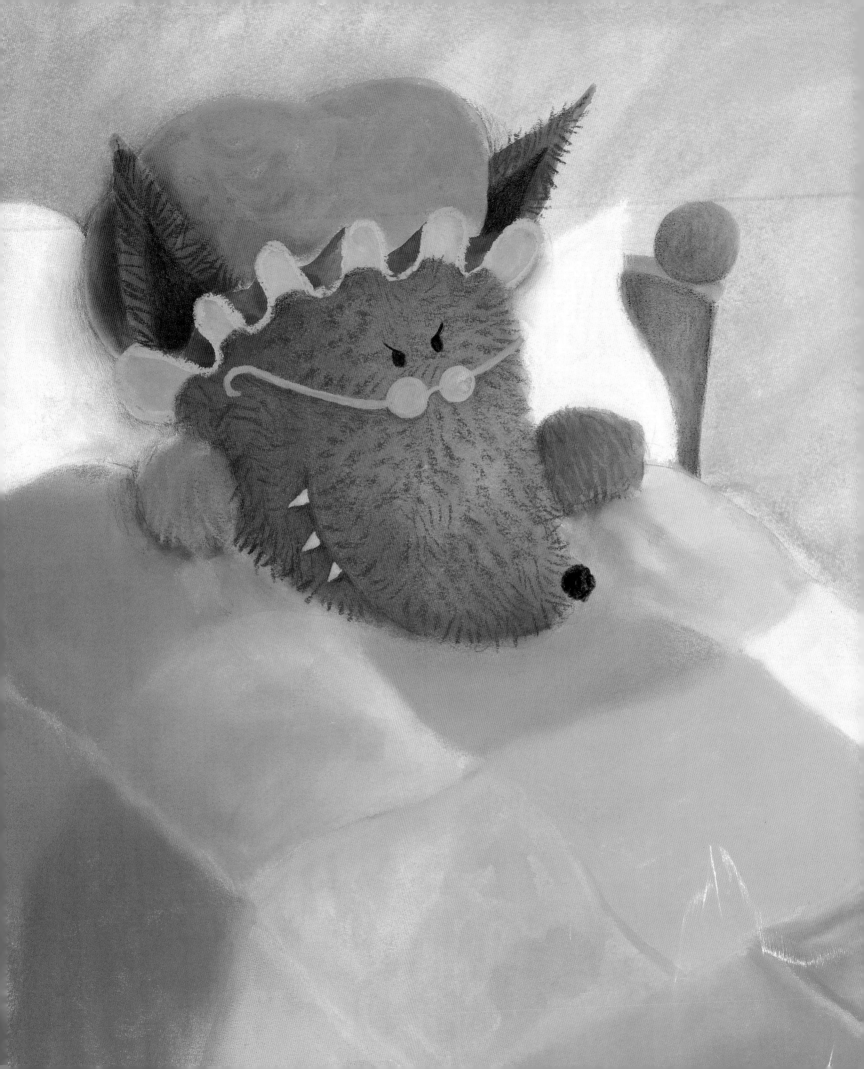

"Grandma must be very sick!" thought
Little Red Riding Hood. "I hope it isn't catching!"

"What big eyes you have, Grandma," she said
as she went over to the bed.

"All the better for seeing you with," the wolf
replied, in the same wobbly voice.

"Grandma, what big ears you have," Little Red Riding Hood added, moving closer.

"All the better for hearing you with," said the wolf, with a toothy grin.

"M...m...my, what big teeth you have, Grandma,"

stuttered Little Red Riding Hood.

"ALL THE BETTER FOR EATING YOU WITH!"

Little Red Riding Hood SCREAMED
and tried to run away. But the hungry
wolf was too fast.

He leaped out of the bed and gobbled
her up in a single, greedy GULP!

A passing woodcutter heard Little Red Riding Hood's scream and ran into the cottage.

When he saw the wolf's enormous belly, he guessed what had happened. He picked up the wolf and shook him hard. Little Red Riding Hood and Grandma flew out of the wolf's mouth.

Luckily, they weren't hurt, but they were VERY cross!

Grandma, Little Red Riding Hood, and the woodcutter chased the wolf into the forest and over the hill.

The embarrassed wolf never came back, and ...

Little Red Riding Hood never

spoke to strangers again.

The End